DAKOTA ALLEN

Captain Fox: An American Legend

D1604521

If there'd be,
Any glory in war, let it rest on men like him,
who went to Hell and came back

Contents

Foreword

Preface

Acknowledgement

Preface

I wrote this book because for starters I love our men and women overseas. They are putting their lives on the line in the name of freedom. The main character was born in 1923 and has fought from Tarawa to Japan and from Korea to Vietnam. He led the charge in WWW and established a beachhead as a one-man army. He lost many friends and family along the way and even got his legs crippled by enemy gunfire. He kept fighting until the end of the war.

The second reason is because of my friends and younger cousin, Brayden. They truly care for me and most have been there for me since my birth. Some guided me through a very dark time in my life. I will treasure them forever. Brayden is my younger cousin and I love him dearly. He has given a lot of ideas for the book and has promised to keep the ideas rolling in. Brayden, I love you.

The final reason is it's an amazing hobby. Words cannot express how much I enjoy writing. Granted I do have my on and off periods, but I have school and life to take care of. This is why this came out as late as it did. However, this book has been meticulously written to be a good read for ages 15 and up. Anyway, I've babbled on long enough, hope you guys enjoy it!
  -Dakota Allen

Acknowledgement

Thank you to my family, my friends, and my younger cousin, Brayden. You truly care for me and most have been there for me since birth. Some of you guided me through a very dark time in my life. Brayden has given a lot of ideas for the book and has promised to keep the ideas rolling in. I love you all.

Prologue

The Letter

    As always during a mission, whoever finds this in the event of my death can turn it into my uncle. My name is Brendan Ryan, I was a Carpenter per-war. I'm not your typical man. I fought the entirety of the battle of Tarawa forward without getting any major wounds. I consider myself lucky. Now we are at the Japanese doorstep.

I'm a paratrooper and we have no reinforcements until the landings on the beach. We're tasked with severing the enemy supply lines. I'm here with a couple of buddies from Basic. Corporal Shepherd, Captain Benson, and Private Thatcher. Always looking over Shepard's Shoulder is Lieutenant Pierson, he's got him on a tight leash. But if Shepherd breaks free, we all get bit. Together we make up Echo Squad. It's about time to jump. It's now or never.

Brendan J. Ryan, 82nd Airborne Division

Chapter 1

Discovery and Heroics

I felt weird. My whole body had been hurting for two days. But this day, it stopped. I heard two Japanese people speaking above me, then it became an argument, then a gunshot and then silence. It was at this moment, I woke up. Then, with inhuman strength, I broke free of my restraints and curb-stomped the Japanese doctor.

I ran to the nearest mirror and looked. I panicked after seeing myself normal, say for fox ears and a tail. But as I was looking for a note on what happened I found my equipment and uniform, and my helmet which had two slits on its sides. Probably for my ears, so I tried it on and it fit perfectly. I then saw a data scroll. I read it and saw room 202, I knew for some reason I was in that room.

Subject 202...injected with yokai serum...deceased...10% humanity

Subject 203...injected with yokai serum...deceased...25% humanity

Subject 204... injected with yokai serum...comatose...50% humanity

Subject 205... injected with yokai serum...pending...95% humanity

It all became clear. My men were being held captive and being turned into monstrosities. I then experienced a humongous headache along with words when I closed my eyes, such as ¨Kill them all¨ or ¨let go of your humanity! ¨ When my headache stopped a few seconds later, I heard at least ten Japanese soldiers behind the door. I pulled my Tommy gun and got ready to fire. They came in with a stretcher.

An American soldier lay on it. He was screaming. "Freeze" I yelled and pumped 100 rounds after kicking away the stretcher. When the smoke cleared, the enemy forces lay dead. I looked towards the soldier. He was quiet, nearly too quiet. When I looked he saw that he had already been injected with the serum, I got him off the stretcher and put him on my back. After about two hours of running through the forest, we ran into an American tank and truck convoy.

We waved them down and the Commander of the lead tank got so scared he shot the MG at least ten times in the air after shining a light at our heads. He ordered something over the radio. A half-track pulled over and got us in. they realized the soldier was turning. He was in severe pain and I gave him morphine. As we headed back to the base, we were intercepted by a Japanese Banzai charge.

The driver automatically got gunned down by an enemy SMG so I crawled over, got onto the Browning, and started firing. I told the infantry and half-tracks over the radio,

"Run to the base and give the order to fire the artillery on my position"

I radioed every tank to cover them while also returning to base. The order was received, reluctantly to say the least. For two hours I defended against waves upon waves of Japanese. The only thing that stopped me was two shots in the shoulder. As I bandaged up I heard the artillery guns firing off in the distance. I knew I was going to die. Everything went black as the artillery came down.

I had been in a coma for 148 days and woke up in an American hospital. I asked the nurse nearby.

CAPTAIN FOX: AN AMERICAN LEGEND

"First of all how's my Girl doing, secondly are there any visitors."

The nurse explained that after the war ended, My Girlfriend, Mary, saw my condition and became a nurse, and she was the nurse. Mary explained that multiple MP's (Military Policemen) were waiting outside. I invited them in. With them was the general of the US army, George Marshall. He explained the war was over, Tokyo was taken and he had been waiting months to give me some things.

He ordered one of his MP's to give him a briefcase, the big one. And he was given one, he gave it to me. I opened it, and sitting there was my M1928, Uniform, Helmet, and a medal of honor. The act of courage I displayed, holding off multiple waves of Japanese Soldiers, not giving up until the bombardment began earned me this award. Also given to me was a purple heart for saving that soldier named PFC Ryan despite being injured myself.

"You're a war hero," he said. I replied,

"I'm no hero, I just did what was necessary to keep my men alive. Also, did you guys ever see a bunker in a forest with a thermite busted door? Because you might want to read any notes you can find." He had a look of horror in his eyes.

"What did you find, captain?" he asked.

I explained, "I was in that bunker. That's how I found PFC Ryan, He and I had been subjected to Inhumane experiments. We weren't the only ones. Those who we did find were dead. Either on a stretcher, on a lab table, or the floor with gunshots put through them. Most of them were... animals or bipedal, but were still animals. All were formerly U.S soldiers. One of them was one of the three plane crash survivors. It was my best friend, Corporal Shepard.

Chapter 2

Pasabandar Landings

Thanks to science and modern medicine, I now know a couple of psychological effects of the experiment done on me back in '46 such as sudden outbursts of violence and anger. But, along with the psychological problems, there were also physical benefits, like increased awareness, speed, agility, and intelligence. Then it was time for my next mission. We were to establish a beachhead at Pasabandar and roll back the Iranian aggression that had terrorized the civilians for 3 years too long.

Alongside me in the boat was my son, Marcus. The Iranians were well dug in but lacked training. Our mission was to take out a few SAM (Surface-to-air missile) turrets near the DZ. We were pinned down and couldn't advance.

"Indigo-Sierra-One-Three-One, do you read, over!" I screamed over the radio.

"Yeah how to copy?"

"I need AC-130 support from grid Alpha-10 to Delta-10, pronto!"

"Copy, enjoy the view boys."

Within minutes the enemy bunkers were reduced to rubble. The enemy was defending fiercely, determined to stop the NATO (North Atlantic Treaty Organization) advance.

Then the tanks arrived, the Karrar MBTs of the Iranian Military Versus the M1A2 Abrams. Obviously, American fire support won. Then from behind us, we saw a blinding light from the USS Nimitz, followed by a shockwave. An ICBM (Intercontinental ballistic missile) destroyed the fleet. We were alone, with no air cover. In essence, we were screwed. As the tanks blew up the bunkers, enemy reinforcements had arrived. Our sergeant, Thomas Ryan, ordered us to fall back. We had Blackhawks on the way. I was determined to hold the line long enough for reinforcements to arrive.

I loaded a box into my LMG as I heard a war cry. As they crested the hill and I unloaded on the wave of enemies. My son stood by me, hitting anyone on the ridge with his M82 anti-tank rifle. Then I heard him scream in pain.

He had been shot right through the chest by a rival sniper. I tended to his wounds as my British friend, Winston, covered us. That's when he started coughing up blood. He wasn't going to make it. He said in between gasps for air

"Please dad, don't let me die here."

I was then filled with grief as he took his last breath right as the helicopter landed. That sadness was quickly replaced by rage. They had killed the one thing I cared about more than my country, and I snapped. I ran towards enemy lines with nothing but a .357 magnum, a combat knife, and unbridled rage. When I came to, I was pointing my magnum at an Arabic soldier, he was begging for mercy.

I looked around and lowered the gun, realizing what I'd done. I had slaughtered the entire Frontline of enemies and was just about to kill their weakest link. I told him to scream. He ran as fast as possible. I went back to the helicopter and headed back to the replacement fleet. But, when I got on, the crew looked at me like I had 16 heads. They would never look at me the same after my massacre.

Chapter 3

One Man Army

As I attended the church service, I couldn't help but listen to the radio, the screaming voices overpowering the pastor. As I walked out, a single helicopter hit the ground. At least 160 bullets and a dud rocket riddled the main body. The rocket pierced the nose and just sat there. The gunner, Lieutenant Herrmann, died in my arms as I unloaded him.

Fully overcome with Rage, I went into the armory and grabbed my M16, a PPQ, and two machetes. Six fragmentation Grenades, 20 medical kits, and four clouds of smoke to call in bombing and artillery strikes. I hopped onto the outbound helicopter. If I had a single sentence to describe the situation, it would be "going into autopilot".

When we reached the Landing Zone I saw them. Winston was holding off at least 300 enemies, 15 others were in defensive positions, but I knew that they couldn't hold for long. I jumped off the helicopter and ran to my comrades. One man, Sergeant Greenmann, was by a tree. His eye hanging out of his socket, firing his Grenade Launcher. I traded my M16 for his grenade launcher and fired 20 grenade launcher rounds at the enemy. The enemy began retreating. I quickly chased them and slit the enemy commander's throat. Big mistake. I felt the first chunks of lead hit me and then went numb. Still filled with adrenaline, I popped the helicopter smoke and yelled for my comrades to, "get to the chopper!"

As the helicopter arrived, they said that there was no more room. I fired a flare gun for another helicopter to arrive. I collapsed and blacked out as the helicopter took off. As I woke up, I realized I was still in the field. Tragedy had struck, the Rescue Black Hawk had crashed, the pilot and door gunner were dead. I went to save Winston, who had been flung from the aircraft. But he choked out his last breath in my arms. I went berserk and killed every insurgent with my bare hands. I saw an allied Chinook land and started running to it, all the while waving my arms around. They got me in and looked shocked. I had about 20 bullet holes and a bayonet stab wound. But I was still walking. I sat down and drifted into unconsciousness.

We had lost so much during the battle, but a more personal loss was my legs. They were crippled during the fighting. The doctor said they're sending me home, and that I'd never walk again.

I begged and pleaded with the doctors to let me fight. The military was my life. They called me "Old Iron".

"Old Iron? Old Iron?! At least I got this far".

They gave me a month to heal, or I would be shipped back. And so that night I crawled from my bed to the wall, only making it 3 feet. The next morning, I crawled 4, and so on, until the pain stopped 29 days in. and so, with my son's help, I walked out of that tent with a new and capable force. Unfortunately, I had to take physical therapy to get used to walking again. At First, I hated it with every fiber of my being. But it slowly grew on me as time went on.

As I was going back to my tent after a session of physical therapy a runner found me and ordered me to head over to defensive position 57 and that there was something big happening. A storm was brewing on the horizon

Chapter 4

Captured

We got word two days before an oncoming attack today. My son, Que, had an M82 Barrett Anti-Material Rifle. I was cleaning my M249s barrel when they came. 10 T72 Armadas, 20 Karrar MBTs, and 1,000 men with air support and heavy weapons, two miles out. I radioed to base,

"MacArthur O.P.D.P(Outer Parameter Defensive Position) number five-seven, we have incoming tanks and air support, requesting assistance immediately". No response. We were out alone in the evening, with enemies incoming 1 mile out.

We figured the least we could do was defend. So we fought, he took on the heavier targets, while I fired on anything firing towards us. While we fought, an enemy sniper must've gotten in a raised position out of our firing arc. As I fired with reckless abandon, Que spotted the enemy and I tried to take the shot with my rifle. It jammed and while I was getting the jammed casing out, I heard another scream In pain.

Que, My own son, had been shot in the Femoral Artery. He was going to die, and he knew it. He gave me a blood-soaked letter to his girl. He told me to give it to her and to tell her

"He was sorry he couldn't make her birthday", before dying. In a Tear filled rage, I tore into enemy troops, Burning them, cutting them, shooting them, even blowing them up until I ran out of ammunition and hope and surrendered. An Arabic soldier walked up to me and hit me in the head with his rifle and I blacked out.

The next thing I knew, I was strapped to a table, and to my left was a whole manner of torture devices. I thought, 'ugh, just like old times, eh. C'mon. ´ I was quickly greeted by the enemy's Chief

Medical Officer. Doctor Muhammad Benson. It's funny because I had served with him during The Second World War.

"We can do this the easy way, you willingly giving the position of the Gerald R Ford, the United States super-carrier, or we torture it out of you," he told me in a friendly voice, like your pediatrician. Then when I did not respond, he slapped me.

Then, he said "You know, we have ways of making your kind talk!" he brandished my weakness. A katana and he poured a can of apricot juice on it.

He put the blunt end on my jugular and dragged along my neck.

"W-well, if I die, I'm dying for freedom!" I told him, He shot me in the leg, mumbled something about filthy Americans, and went to answer the knock on the door. He opened it and Mary was tied to a table a foot away from me. She was a code talker.

"Finally someone at the very least competent."

He pulled the same trick on her, and she said "go to hell, traitor." He pulled a gun and shot her in the chest. At that moment, I was filled with unbridled rage. I broke free of the restraints and killed that monster. I took his gun and went on a rampage. Afterward, I grabbed the katana and put it in my bag. Mary was bleeding badly and I grabbed her and ran 20 miles back to base.

Mary had lost a lot of blood, and we were of the same blood type, so I gave her a transfusion of two liters. But I didn't take into account that my DNA was altered and that she would be of the same species as me in two to three days.

Chapter 5

Fragile Peace

With hostilities still going on, the war ended when the leader of the Iranian Army and his command staff were killed in a bombing raid by British forces, the president had to give in to demands of ¨surrender now or Tehran will be bombed into oblivion¨. Hell, if the limeys just kept quiet, we could have kept the war going for another year or so...but they deserve the victory credit.

As I got onto the boat, I wondered how fast I would adjust to civilian life. But one thing is for sure. I'm going to make a grand speech in two years. As the boat departed, I had a gut feeling that I shouldn't head back, cause in two years, something horrific would happen, but I just ignored it assuming it was superstition. With Mary, now with the same abnormal features as me, we held hands as the ships sailed off to the Suez Canal, and from there Rome, and then home.

I lived a life of peace. I began a training camp on my farm for new recruits. Things appeared to be going well. Pollution was at an all-time low, birth rates were up. The only problem was that I was something of a national celebrity. I was called to do speeches daily. But there was one, two years after the war which I said ¨yes¨ to.

As I prepared to step onto the podium, I got a bit nervous and flipped through my script. I was ready. I stepped onto the podium and began my speech.

"War...War never changes. In 1776, this great nation accepted that armed conflict was the only way to preserve our rights to life, liberty, and the pursuit of happiness. If our founding fathers could only see us now..."

"From Antietam to Amiens, Okinawa to Tehran, we have fought. And now, Russia is at our doorstep. Democracy itself is under threat of annihilation. That is why today, July fourth, 2023, we gather together to honor the completion of Bunker 1776."

"This sprawling fallout shelter may have been designed by BFG International, but it was built by you-" suddenly I heard a 45. Pistol fired twice, and the next thing I knew I was on the ground. In severe pain, I told my wife ¨take care of our daughter...¨ I trailed off as I fell into Unconsciousness. They put me in a cryogenic chamber, seemingly saving me for later, and for 17 years, I stayed that way. Until one day when I heard,

"Cryogenic Stasis Suspended."

In the room were two strangers, one looked familiar.

"Are you sure this is the right pod? Is this even the right bunker?!"

"I'm positive."

"Alright, opening in three...two...one..."

I was strapped in so when they opened it and I saw one reach into their pocket, I was screaming, ¨please, please don't kill me¨ then I saw the familiar face. It was my son, Que Joseph Ryan. I started to experience parasomnia. I saw my son on the day he died, covered in blood, coughing up the stuff. Telling me his last words.

I was shaking, stammering and hyperventilating. ¨Que, don't die on me, please! Please!!¨ my restraints came loose and I fell, crying and shaking. I felt a warm hand on my shoulder and Que came to comfort me.

"Dad, I'm alright, c'mon, let's get you out here."

"No, this has to be one of my PTSD fits, this has to be a dream. I watched you bleed out in our foxhole. Just let me live in peace, please!"

"Dad, Look at me"

I looked, tears streaking down my face. It was him, he was basically the same, except with lots of scars and a beard. I got up with some assistance and hugged my son. I was so glad he was alive.

"What happened to you?" I asked.

"After you were captured, I was found by a group of scavengers. They turned me into the Afghan militia, where they performed surgery and a little bit of black magic. I wanted to return home, they said 'you're supposed to be dead.' So one night, during the chaos of the Great War, I got on a fishing boat and sailed to Baltimore, I was shot at, beaten, stabbed. But I came all this way for you. See, I had heard rumors that you were locked away in stasis in a bunker. So I went looking through West Virginia, searching every bunker I found. Until I found the location of Bunker 1776."

As I was about to speak, I heard the distant sound of tank treads and at least 30 armored trucks. Ques's eyes widened and he handed me an anti-tank gun and a box of ammo.

"Get into positions, raiders are coming one mile out!"

Chapter 6

Total War

As we got into positions, I immediately noticed that the surrounding landscape was a desertic powder color, the earth tainted by the Nuclear War that had happened about 17 years ago. The next thing I noticed was 400 men in position behind fallen trees and rocks. A man stood 500 feet ahead behind no cover and no escape if we shot him. In his hand was a megaphone. 4 tanks, all of unknown origin, sat with barrels aimed. The man put the megaphone to his mouth and spoke.

"Listen, we can do this the easy way, you giving us the Fox boy or the hard way, we kill you all."

"We would rather be killed than give you our father."

"So be it. All units ope-"

Suddenly an explosion rocked the enemy battalion. A low sweeping F14 Tomcat strafed the enemy infantry as it pulled up. The tanks were destroyed by the bombs and rockets as more Fighters flew overhead. I took aim at the man with the megaphone and pulled the trigger.
   The man collapsed and died. A Bell UH-1 Huey flew in and picked us up. The few infantrymen who survived scattered. I couldn't help but say "I love the smell of napalm in the morning" as the helicopter flew off into the sunset

towards Flatwoods. When we got to what Que called the Citadel, I saw my wife, Mary, walking towards the helicopter.

"I see you extracted the...Brendan? My god, Brendan, how did you make it out alive!?" She looked shocked. I said,

"I'm immortal, remember. I can only be killed by an apricot-lined dagger."

She ordered a Private to take me to the Class I barracks while my quarters were made ready and to give me fresh fatigues, helmet, and the custom MX1 Garand off the shelf.

"Well, regardless, I'm promoting you to your previous rank; Major. Your first mission begins tomorrow, meet me at 0830 hours for the details. AT EASE, HUSBAND!"

I followed the Private to the barracks and believe it or not, he opened the door for me. He showed me to my bunk. He explained that the top bunk was a former soldier, Captain Steven Haden. But he was killed in action holding the border.

"What happened?"

"Oh, I apologize. When a man named Brendan Ryan, AKA Captain Fox died, it was discovered that it was a Russian spy who assassinated him. That sparked a nuclear war. After the radiation settled two groups came to power. The Raiders and the Settlers. The Raiders were the people who invaded with no provocation. We keep losing ground. We are surrounded, outgunned, and outnumbered. Unless we can pull a victory out of thin air, we've lost this war."

  "Captain Fox. Now, that's a name I haven't heard in a long time."

"I think my dad knows him. He said he was dead."

19

"Oh, he's not dead. Not yet."

"You know him?"

"Well of course I know him. He's me."

"You're Captain Fox?! Sir, you were my hero in the years leading up to the war, you were everyone's hero in my hometown of Sutton. They erected a statue of you in the town square, but the raiders destroyed it when they invaded."

I reached into my suitcase and pulled a large case out. I quickly grabbed a knife and opened it. I etched my Signature onto my M1 carbines Receiver and handed it off to him.

"Consider this a collectible. Be careful, this bad boy is just around 100 year's old, original everything."

I left a shocked expression and hopefully a lasting impression on the soldier. He continued giving me everything I needed, calling me "Captain" instead of the standard "Sir". I told him it wasn't necessary, but he insisted it was, he retorted that I was his hero. I went to sleep about 1 hour later as troops were beginning to settle down for a good night's rest.

Chapter 7

Battle for Sutton

Reveille began at 0700 hours and I got up first, did my morning routine, and raised the two flags at the entrance; the West Virginian settler's flag and the 50-star American flag. After that, I lifted weights and took a five-mile jog around the Citadel's walls, observing the activities of the farmers outside tending to their crops and animals. At 0825 hours I walked into the briefing room to see my unit. It definitely wasn't what I was expecting.

For starters they were unfit, most were skinny with no muscular build. They were also white as ghosts. Mary pulled me aside and told me that they were eager recruits that had just come back from a scouting mission of the town of Sutton. Some just up and left and some Christians have even turned atheists after seeing a pile of rotting bodies in the open, covered with flies being thrown into a pit at least 6 feet deep

I was to lead 400 men of the 77th Armored Infantry Battalion to retake Sutton while these men recovered. If we succeeded in this mighty endeavor we would stand a chance against the raiders. Que would be going with us but we would break off 2 miles from Sutton. Our orders were to support the Ques Battalion. We were a proud unit, we changed the war for West Virginia. The Appalachian Devil Dogs.

When we got to the bridge leading to Sutton we took the enemy by surprise. The ones on the bridge were quick to surrender. The private who I had given the M1 carbine, Known as Josh, took point and began creeping up on a group of sandbags, MX1 Ready.

Suddenly a burst of Gunfire erupted from the building. One bullet grazed his helmet while he was taking cover. I ordered a mortar team to aim for the windows that erupted in gunfire. The mortar was let loose and the side of that building went up in smoke, which revealed the MG-15 team. We let loose with everything we had. After about 15 seconds I gave the order to hold fire. The MG Team was reduced to steaming heaps of flesh.

We started to advance to the town square but something seemed off. I ordered my men to stop and gave the hand signal to follow my lead. Suddenly, I heard five clicks and ordered my men to get to cover. As I got behind cover after everyone else, a bullet impacted my helmet but bounced off. It was a trap, five machine gun teams and two snipers were shooting at the building we were behind. We were pinned down and had no escape. For the first time in years, I prayed. Prayed for someone to save us.

As soon as I said "amen" 30 people dressed in rags burst through the doorway to the tavern holding shotguns and rifles.

"The revolution has begun!" one cried

"Viva La Resistance!" Shouted another.

They burst into households and shot the raiders dead. They never stood a chance. We took down the raider flag and burned it. We then replaced it with the American and Settler flag. I felt a great sense of patriotism. I look over to my son and his eye is hanging out of his socket. I told him to see a medic and as he walked off he said "Eh, look better with an eye patch! ¨ We had a good laugh and even the general chuckled.

That night as I wrote in my logbook in my new quarters in the basement of the old tavern, I got a knock on my bedroom door. I told them to come in and the same lady who was with Que when I was rescued had shown up.

"Hey dad"

¨Hi- wait. You're not who I think you are. Maria? ¨

"In the flesh"

I quickly stood up and gave her a hug. She said she was in the air force as a pilot of an A-10 warthog. I was happy my family was back together. Suddenly I saw movement behind her.

"Who is that behind you?"

"It is my daughter, Alexandra. Say hi, Alex."

She stood beside the wall and waved. In the cutest voice I ever did hear, she said "Hi Grand-pappy"

"Who is the lucky guy?" I asked

¨Lenard Luther, he's a carpenter.¨

I smiled, thinking back to me and my brother, who died when I was 10. He was stabbed to death while protecting me from my alcoholic parents. He would always welcome me into his workshop to paint the furniture that he would make with scrap wood from old shanties and then put them up for sale. I have to confess. I joined the army, not because of Pearl Harbor. I was angry, sure, but it was to prove to my parents that I wasn't a mistake, an opinion they took to their graves. I never told anyone because they left too much of a scar on my memories and I feared retaliation. I'm sorry if I let you down, Buck.

Chapter 8

Fight for the Citadel

    At around 11:45 that night, I abruptly woke up to an extended shudder along with alarms and sirens. 9 men had taken cover next to my bed, one of them having a wound on their shoulder which was being treated. I was confused as I just woke up. Then it clicked. It was an artillery barrage. A soldier spoke up,

"Not to worry, sir. This is just how they say 'Have a good weekend! ´ It usually lasts anywhere from 40-50 minutes, but it is just about to reach an hour this time. Besides, if an attack does come, Wade Airfield is within range to send some of our flyboys over and blow the enemy to Kingdom Come."

Then the radio next to my bed, devoid of radio chatter came to life.

¨AW32 TO DISPATCH! ¨

¨Go ahead AW32.¨

¨WE HAVE MULTIPLE CLASS A, B, C, D, AND E FIRES HERE! THEY JUST FIREBOMBED THE AIRFIELD! SEND ALL THE AMBULANCES AND ENGINES YOU GOT, BECAUSE I GUARANTEE IT WON'T BE ENOUGH! ¨

¨10-4, sending emergency personnel your way.¨

I was scared because my daughter's barracks were there. I wanted to get out there and see if my daughter was alive. Then my wife's voice came over the PA system.

"Attention all personnel, we have enemies coming in Ten miles out. 1,000 men, 10 tanks, and 20 Anti-Tank guns being towed by trucks. Get to your defensive positions immediately!"

I quickly ran up the stairs and held the door for the soldiers who were taking cover in my office. I ran to the radio room and called for air support from another airfield, Tucker Army Airfield. Complete radio silence. I assumed they had been bombed too. I quickly ran towards the door to the armory, dodging artillery shells along the way. At last, I reach the door, open it and run to my locker. In it are an M249 LMG, 4 Fragmentation Grenades, an M82 AT Rifle, and finally a flare gun.

I left the sniper in the locker. It reminded me of how I failed my son that cold Arabian night. Some nights I can still hear his moans in agony as he laid there bleeding out. I ran out, got to the wall defenses, and set up the bipod. I heard a click and the sky lit up with enemy tracer rounds. A Private ran up to me, his hand on his helmet

"Sir, you are company commander now, Miller is dead. What are your orders?!"

"Fire At the origins of those tracers. Understood?"

"Yes sir!"

Suddenly I heard the wailing of a Stuka´s Jericho Trumpet. Except it was getting louder and there were more of them. Before I could react, an explosion behind me knocked me forward and I blacked out after hitting my head on the road.

When I came to, an enemy soldier was walking up to me from the fire and flames. He poured a can of apricot juice on his knife. He crouched next to me and set the knife tip on my chest, slowly plunging it into my chest.

"So we have Captain Fox, a former war hero, being beaten by his equal." the soldier remarked, stabbing the knife deeper into my chest. By this point, the pain was really starting to get to me. "I'd hate to break it to you pal, but the game was rigged from the start. Now there is no way out of where you are going."

I pulled my pistol out of my holster and remarked, "If that's true I'll see you there!" and blasted him twice. He fell to the ground dead. I began to blackout again.

"Sargent! Over here!" a man echoed. It was a medic who had found me. "Don´t worry, Sir. The attack has been repelled. You're safe." he explained. Right before I blacked out, I heard him say "Get me a Goddamn stretcher, Pronto!

Chapter 9

Beginning of the winter offensive

Unbeknownst to me and quite possibly the raiders at the time the war had turned in our favor during that battle. We had destroyed their best tank crews and troops during the battle for The Citadel. The Raiders, however, put a rather large dent in our forces. One that we would need to fill rapidly. My unit, the 701starmored infantry had proved themselves worthy of battle at the Battle of Sutton and at The Citadel.

When I woke up, I was being checked on by Mary and Doctor Amari, a doctor who worked for the United States Marine Corps during the war in Iran.

"Hey, the General is Finally Awake. You've been out for a week." He Smiled.

I began to panic, asking where my daughter was. I remembered 12 minutes before the bombing she said she was going back to Wade Airfield and it usually took 10 minutes to get there from The Citadel.

"Don't worry Sir, she's alright. But she did something that will earn her the Congressional Medal of Honor and her own squadron."

"What did she do?" I asked, curious of the deed my daughter had done.

"During the bombing, she took an A-10 Warthog and took out the second wave of B-52 Stratofortress with heat-seeking missiles and the 30 mm cannon. In total, she shot down 12 with engines burning and damaged 13 to the point they had to turn back. Because of her efforts, the Raider Army Air Corps had to turn back and call off the strike, saving hundreds if not thousands of lives."

I couldn't help but smile knowing my daughter was a war hero. I was once considered one, but not by the press during Vietnam. They saw me as a brute because whenever the VCs would attack from the Bushes, I would send in men with flamethrowers to burn down the battlefield. If I found a Vietcong Tunnel System Entrance, I would pour gasoline down the hole and light a match and sometimes I heard screaming.

My strategy was effective and we could've turned the tide, but because of all the negative publicity, I was shipped back to America. I still resent the US Government for that. Because of them, we lost that war, and many men were left behind.

As I went through the course of recovery, I started to notice a slight pain in my chest which started to get worse as the days went by. On the first day, one part of my brain said to see a doctor, the other said to keep going with recovery and walk it off. On the tenth day I went to see a doctor. Turns out it was rot on the wound that the enemy general gave me. The doctor put me in hospital for 3 days on constant antibiotics.

When I got out, The Settler Armed Forces was in a state of disarray. The raiders had cratered the airstrip with 5,000 lbs. bombs and had destroyed 210 of our Modern Planes. Nearly 3,000 men were killed, including most of the Settler Air Force command staff. 1/6th of those men earned the posthumous Medal of Honor for actions above and beyond the call of duty, such as Arnold Canter.

He was only 15 when he died manning his Anti-Aircraft gun, shooting down 3 bombers in a single magazine, as well as 2 bombs aimed directly at the ammunition depot. The depot survived the battle and many lives were saved.

After going through rehab I was called back for an assault on the city of Berkeley Springs, less than 140 miles from the Raider Capital of West Virginia, Monongah. Aerial recon showed the small town had 20 infantry battalions, some 100 artillery guns in place, 20 Pillboxes, 2 tank regiments with troops and officers included, and a super-heavy tank. The tank model was unknown, but it looked like a Bigger British Churchill Heavy Tank from WW2.

We had 2 days to prepare for the line. We had tank support and 2,000 men already at the front. Estimated losses were 5,000 men dead and 8,000 injured. Our forces consisted of 20 mortar teams, 120 artillery batteries in place, 20 tanks made up of 8 T110E5 Super-Heavies and 12 M60 Patton's, and 15,000 men with 20,000 in reserve. There was a 48 percent chance of failure on this mission.

The plan was a frontal assault. We would encircle the city's outer defensive perimeter and slowly stream over the Berkeley Springs bridge, starving the enemy into submission. We would reduce the city to dust if we had to, but that was not the plan we had in mind.

As dawn came on the day we shipped out, I woke up at 0600 hours and got ready. I put on my WW2 BDU set from my glory days and grabbed a shoulder backpack. In it, I put an ammo box of 45. ACP, 2 canteens, 2 MREs, A Radio, 3 Tommy gun Stick mags, and 4 M1911 magazines. That was about 94 LBS of equipment on my back, but I managed. Outside my bag, I had a KA-BAR knife, a Colt M1911 pistol, an m1a1 bazooka, and finally my Tommy gun. Before we left I visited the chaplain and asked for him to pray with me. He did and I boarded the truck, crossing myself as I did.

Chapter 10

Reuniting at Berkeley Springs.

As we drove the 200 miles to the front, I saw many things. But the worst thing I saw wasn't the destruction, it wasn't the bodies. It was the missing posters made by kids in every town, city, and village with the names of the Prisoners of War and the Missing in Action of that town. They all said the same thing. "Please Come Home Daddy" or "Please Come Home Mommy" with another message like "we love you" or "we miss you."

That honestly made me cry. If only they knew that 90% of the POWs get executed somewhere down the line or are worked to death. Mid-thought someone tapped me on the shoulder.

"Sir, are you okay?"

I turn around and see a somewhat familiar face. A face I hadn't seen in over a century.

"I'm sorry, I feel like I know you, but I'm not sure."

The man spoke up

"Oh. I'm sorry, you probably don't remember me after all these years. Let me give you a hint. 'I won't let you hurt my baby brother'"

I sat there in shock. It clicked in my mind that it was Buck. He was alive.

"B-Buck? You're alive."

"I've been in hiding, I faked my own death and tried to get you out as well, but Mom and Dad kicked me out at gunpoint."

I snapped, yelling and crying.

"All this time I've been writing letters to you and burning them, trying to contact you. Do you know how many times I've tried to commit suicide over the past century because I wanted to be with you again? 34 times, two times during a war. But my lucky ass either jams the gun or dulls the knife, or the enemy misses the shots. Or maybe it's because I CAN'T DIE! I just won't die."

The air was so still in that truck you could hear a pin drop. Buck was tearing up and then proceeded to do something I haven't had from him in years. He Hugged me. The last time I had that was about two minutes before he "Died." I just let it happen and was truly happy for the first time in a good long while.

We came to a stop at the front about two minutes later. The area was covered in countless white crosses. A soldier explained that a good number of them were killed with gas. The last shipment they got was 2 weeks ago. This convoy had gas masks, troops, ammo, and everyday essentials. The charge would begin at 12:00 PM Preceded by a 2-hour long artillery barrage with a multitude of shells. High Explosive, Anti-tank, Gas, Smoke, White Phosphorus. You name it, they fired it randomly at the enemy line.

As the artillery came to a stop I yelled,

"Fix bayonets and prepare your gas masks!"

I heard the countless sounds of men fixing bayonets onto their rifles and shotguns, followed by the sound of men putting on fresh gas masks. I looked at my watch, it was 11:59:45. 15 seconds. I pulled out my whistle as I did not

CAPTAIN FOX: AN AMERICAN LEGEND

have a gas mask. I was willing to face the gas as I was basically immortal.

As soon as I blew the whistle and the tanks drove over us, they were hit with MG42 and M249 fire in the towers sitting on opposite sides of the bridge leading into the city. The second whistle followed and we charged. We just needed to take out the towers and we would be relatively fine. I was taking hits but I kept running, eventually making it to the right tower.

"Defenders of Berkeley Springs Bridge, I am giving you one chance to surrender. If you refuse, you all get sent home to your wife or mom in a pinewood box or an urn."

I heard footsteps and 14 men, all conscripts came out of the first tower with their weapons away and their hands up. There was only one defender who did not surrender. He was shot immediately upon entering. He turned out to be a 15-year-old kid who had been brainwashed by the raider's propaganda. I went to the let tower and tried the same trick.

"Defenders of Berkeley Springs Bridge, I am giving you one chance to surrender. If you refuse, you all get sent home to your wife or mom in a pinewood box or an urn."

I was met with a burst of machine gun fire at the door. Their accuracy was shit. They kept missing me. I fired back with my Thompson submachine gun, gunning them down in an instant.

Suddenly I hear the distant sound of tank treads. I looked out the window and to my horror, the super-heavy, two Panzer III's and two ISU-152s were driving down a side road. I Ran downstairs and yelled for them to get down, right as the super-heavy fired. A flash of blue light hit right where I was in the tower when I spotted them. This was no ordinary tank. It had a 15-foot railgun. I knew what I had to do.

I charged at the tanks. I parkour my way up the Churchill Super-heavies hull and kicked open the unlocked hatch. There were no other tanks; they had split up. I shot all 6 crew members dead and took control of the vehicle. I ordered 5 men to man the thing. A driver, 2 machine gunners, a gunner, and a radio operator. one of the ISU-152's, in typical Russian fashion, charged at our line, and right as the side was visible and I ordered the gunner to fire.

A loud bang echoed through the hull. But then we heard a massive explosion. The enemy tank had blown up spectacularly. A Panzer III tried desperately to pierce our armor with its 75mm gun. The shell just bounced back and hit the tank in the front. We had a good laugh as the ISU backed off. We let them go for now.

Within 2 days we took the city with only 1,000 casualties, 13 times less than the estimated total. We took over 10,000 men prisoner and killed the rest. We captured the super heavy and the artillery guns. It's a shame we took the Churchill apart, kept the gun, and melted down the rest. But that gun would be a valuable asset in the years to come. The Raiders were now officially on the defensive. The wings of an eagle have been broken and Major Whitley's orders are clear.

"Burn Monongah to ash."

Chapter 11

Assault on Castle Thorpe

About two months after the battle of Berkeley Springs, I was called to duty once again. We were to attack Castle Thorpe. My son would be a part of the assault. I wouldn't, I was considered by the high command to be "too valuable of an asset to lose".

On the day of the assault, I was at the command post two miles from the front. Que was with Josh, as part of the 5th wave. The area had turned into a muddy mess with the worst rainfall in years and the constant shelling. As I peered through the binoculars, I saw raiders and settlers floating face first in the mud-filled shell craters. I zoomed in and saw their company commander getting ready to lead the charge.

I heard a faint whistle and they climbed up the trench and into the Kill zone. I could only watch in absolute horror as the second wave fell a mere 15 meters from the trench, and some 45 meters away from being out of the machine gun's depression angle.

I heard a couple comments behind me like "Oh Jesus Christ." or "My son was in that wave" I heard someone vomit as they saw the carnage. The third wave was just as bad if not worse. Men were using bodies as shields. But it was all in vain, they died anyway. The fourth wave gained some traction, getting 15 meters away from cover.

I shed a tear thinking of what might happen to my son's wave. But it wasn't what I thought. A few men including my son actually got to safety. We sent men to reinforce their line. Suddenly a bright light broke through the clouds. It wasn't the sun. It was an intercontinental ballistic missile.

"GET DOWN!" someone yelled.

Next thing I knew I was on the ground amidst the rubble of the observation post. I got up and peered out the window. A green mist had covered the area. The radiation levels were high, indicating a nuclear explosion had just occurred. I had to find my son, fast. I suited up in the newly designed T-100 Armored Hazmat Suit and grabbed a 1911 and a knife.

The bastards had actually done it. They had actually gone and used the ultimate terminator. As I got closer to the blast site, I started getting shot at by wounded raiders trying to pull their way to the elevator. They were met with deadly accurate pistol fire. I picked up a Model 1897 Shotgun and an M16 and entered the elevator, heading to the second floor.

The Instant the elevator door opened I was under heavy gunfire. I took out the machine gunner first with a slug from the 1897 and then a man running up to me with a machete with the same weapon. Then I heard a man say,

"Hold Fire! This one's mine"

I look up and see David Thorpe. The Raiders Dictator. He was dressed in a uniform reminiscent of a Nazi Officer Uniform. His left hand was on his holster and his right was on the rail. He was an evil man, one who oftentimes killed men personally after taunting them a bit and took their heads as trophies.

"If it isn't my old friend, the frozen TV dinner. The last time we met, you were cozying up to the peas and apple cobbler. Let me tell you a secret. Your wife had your twins shortly after I came to power. I sent spies to watch over them, because I had plans for them. Both joined the SAF. But I killed the boy, I believe his name was....Timothy? He and his unit were surrounded by my soldiers. He was a runner. I fired the shot that eventually killed him. Shame, he was a good kid too."

I was shocked, but that was quickly replaced by rage.

"You are murdering, kidnapping psychopaths. I've heard stories about you. And let me tell you that when I finally die, I hope to go to hell. Just so I can kill you all over again."

We got into a firefight, every time I would get a clear shot on him, he would dodge it and fire back. I worked my way up the stairs leading to him. When I got up to him he hit me in the face with the but of his rifle, knocking out a few of my teeth. He ran like the coward he was to the elevator. I followed him and took care of the rest of the raiders along the way.

As soon as I got to the 3rd floor, I saw my son getting shot and wrestled Thorpe onto the ground. He swung and I caught it. He used his hand-to-hand combat abilities to push me off him and get me on my knees. He pulled out a .700 Nitro Express revolver and put it to my head.

Right as I heard the gun click as it jammed, I heard 3 gunshots, and the Raider Commander Stumbled. Que had pulled out his revolver and was just about to take the final shot when a rocket exploded and sent shrapnel into my boy. He hit his head on the steel bars and passed out. I quickly got him out of the cage and slung him over my shoulder.

I looked out the hole in the wall and saw a bunch of settler soldiers using flamethrowers and machine guns to mop the enemy reinforcements up. I saw my wife standing below, directing fire.
   "Get clear" I yelled as I jumped.

I landed from 160 feet up, feet first, and sprained my left kneecap. I ordered the medics to treat Que before me. They loaded him onto an ambulance after determining he'd need surgery pronto and took him to the Citadel Medical Ward. A medic then checked on me, he yelled for a newly designed "I.H.E.I" I didn't understand what that meant so I asked. It meant Instant Healing Emergency Injection. I asked,

"Why not use that on my son?"

"We Can't Use an I.H.E.I to get shrapnel, we need to give him emergency surgery. Even with surgery, he has only a 34.9% chance of survival. So be ready to say your goodbyes.

The surgery went well, but he was in a coma for about a week on life support and another without the vent. My wife and I volunteered to give our blood.

"But the Transfusion might kill him, if not alter his DNA." The doctors said, but I was persistent.

"It's worth a shot. Are you willing to let my son die or not?"

The doctor finally gave in. He hooked me and my wife up to a machine to draw my blood via needles. He left us for 30 minutes and after about 25 minutes I began to pass out. Another doctor checked in on us and disconnected the needles to my wife and me. They then took us to a buffet where we ate like royalty.

Chapter 12

Battle over Morgantown

During the time we were getting our blood drawn, a massive air battle was taking place over the raider city of Morgantown. We had captured several modern aircraft during our winter and spring offensives, including a multitude of F-18 Hornets and 45 B-52 Stratofortresses. But there was a bigger prize at hand. A chance at ending the war quickly.

At 0847 hours a Cessna Recon Aircraft took photos of a freshly built industrial complex 2 miles from the city of Morgantown. To hear it from them, it was massive, containing dozens of oil reserve tanks and armor plants just waiting to be bombed. And so it was. Every available plane in the Settler Air Forces arsenal was scrambled and sent to the target. Even biplanes got in on the action, but most were shot down before they reached the target.

My daughter's squadron "The Winged Hussars" was part of the assault. Entirely made up of A-10 Warthogs, the squadron spearheaded the assault on the enemy industrial complex. These were Maria's words, so don't quote me,

"The B-52s were at 75% throttle so they were lagging behind. It was our mission to clear the path for the Bombers. The instant we came over Morgantown we had missile locks on us and Flak filled the skies. We had to fly low to prevent being shot down. I gave the order to fire at will when we were 200 yards from the oil refinery of the industrial complex. The rockets and the bullets set off a chain reaction that blew up the refinery.

"I yanked back on the stick at 100 feet, flying through debris as I did. Suddenly I heard a Transmission from Hussar Two. 'I've been hi-' I look over to see his plane burst into flames and disintegrate mid-air after being hit by a heat-seeker from an F-14. I pulled a 9-G turn to face the Tomcat who killed my wingman, almost blacking out as I did. He was caught mid-turn and I lit him up like a Christmas tree. The explosion was spectacular."

"But then my plane started to shake, Hussar Five Pulled up alongside me and exclaimed 'Jesus Christ, Hussar Leader, you've got a hole in your right wing!' I looked over and sure enough, a Hole about one foot in diameter had formed in my right-wing. I had to return to base. I rallied my squadron and we headed back to base, our job done."

I was proud of my daughter and my son was getting better, things were coming back to normal. Except for one thing. My son, based on my observation, was slowly turning into a werewolf. The changes were subtle at first, such as flicking of the ears and a faster heartbeat.

Then, one day while I was in the waiting room, I heard him howling in pain. I tried to get the doctors to let me in, pleading, screaming but they didn't budge. To my shock I felt my jaw start to crack. It was turning into a snout. I felt my ears begin to become more foxlike and my hair started to grow on my back and arms. Finally after a couple seconds of trying to control it and tears running down my eyes. My wife calmed me down with four simple words.

"Brendan, I'm right here."

After that, I returned to normal and they finally let me in. As I walked up to the window looking into his room and the screams got louder I heard him say,

"I don't want to turn. I want to stay Human. Please God, Help me."

I put my hand on the window and he looked over, his eyes bloodshot. I quickly went in and held him like a baby comforting him, cradling him like I did when he was an Infant.

¨It's going to be alright, mom and I gave you our blood. You'll still remain in control.¨ I was visibly shaken and my eyes were bloodshot. He could sense something was wrong. I saw him looking, and sat down. I told him events that unfolded in the lobby.

¨I got angry at a doctor, he wouldn't let me see you. My jaw started to extend into a snout and I felt my nails extending. My ears grew a bit more fur and the hair on my back also turned into fur. I had to fight the urge to kill him. He let me in soon after. But still, I nearly lost control and the last time I did that, I massacred an entire Middle Eastern village. I thought I was human after the war in Iran ended, but, when I get a bit angry, my fox ears and tail come out. I can only fear what happens when I lose control. I'm sorry Que, if you blow your top, you'll lose control.¨

He just cried and cried and cried. I held him until he fell asleep. After that I laid him back down in his bed and tucked him in. I missed doing that so much. I just had to do it again.

Chapter 13

Captured Again.

I tried helping my son any way I could after his discharge. He began talking about training his mind and body to not lose control all that often. I was convinced it wouldn't work. But I would learn it does work on the seventh day of his training when he told me,

"Strap Me down into this chair. It's embedded into the concrete so don't worry about me breaking free."

I strapped him down and placed the metal cuffs on his hands and legs and he told me to play a tape on the table. I put the tape into the VCR player. As the video played of raider propaganda footage, he began to sweat and wince as he started to turn. I noticed his nails beginning to extend and his nose began to become more square and darker in color. He began to tear up as his teeth began to elongate and sharpen as a tail began to form.

"I–I'm sorry for being so stupid d–dad"

I comforted him as his muscles began to tense and expand and his clothes ripped. I could tell he was in severe pain. His jaw pushed forward a bit and he screamed as it popped.

"It's OK bud, I'm Right Here"

"L-Love" He tried to say before letting out a deep growl as his jaw extended into a snout and his eyes turned a Golden Yellow color. His dark brown fur, in little splotches at this point, began to expand to cover his entire body as he tried to break free of the restraints. As soon as the cuffs began to buckle the video ended and he came to. He whimpered and tried to speak but he could only say a couple words at a time.

"Monster, Dad."

I approached him and he growled. I stopped but kept going.

"STAY BACK! Might hurt you."

I finally got to him and wrapped him in a hug,

"Bud, you're not a monster. You have an issue, sure. But I can assure you, you're no monster."

He walked over to the table and grabbed a fresh set of clothes. He went into the bathroom and changed back into his human form, afterwards he changed into his fresh set of clothes. After this, he hugged me and told me he was sorry.

"For what?" I asked. I was legitimately confused on why he said sorry.

"For being stupid for one, and for two, you having to see that."

"It's fine bud, I'm willing to help you anytime you need it."

After his training Que and I were called to active service. The briefing began at 0700 hours. I and my unit were to attack the city of Morgantown and liberate its people who were being used as forced laborers for mining. Que and the 76th armored battalion would attack the city of Grafton instead of supporting the infantry. I thought this idea was stupid, but this decision was made last second by high command.

By 0800 hours, a large blizzard had moved in, and by the time we got to the trucks, snow had blanketed the ground by 2 inches. As we took the 1 hour 30 minute drive to the battlefield, the men in my truck sang "Screaming Eagles" and "82nd all the way", at least our versions of the hit Sabaton songs.

About one hour 25 minutes into our drive we came across a raider scouting party, we quickly hopped out and they tried to surrender. But, their markings were different. Turns out they were the Raiders equivalent of the Wafer SS of Nazi Germany Known as "Death Division." one of my men pulled out an M16 and put it to the head of the scout party's commander. Right before he pulled the trigger, I pulled my pistol.

"Listen here private, If you shoot this man, I will be your judge, jury and executioner. Do you understand?"

He pulled the gun away and I laid into him.

"You are an absolute imbecile. I understand you want to kill raiders, but we are a democracy, everyone gets a fair trial if they surrender. Do you want us to look like the bad guys? Next time you do a stunt like that, I will court Marshall you. Understood private?

"Y-yes sir!" the private stuttered.

After that incident we walked to the frontline and we got into the trench, ready to kick ass and chew bubblegum, and we were all out bubblegum. The order to charge was given at 1100 hours and we charged. We were met with MG fire from the enemy trench. I took out the MG-42 with a couple grenades. About halfway across the field, I heard the sound of a doodlebug bomb coming in hot. There was no cover so I kept fighting. Eventually the V-1 came down, killing most of my men and knocking me out.

43

As I woke up I saw an enemy countercharge coming in so I grabbed my 1911 and started shooting. I took out 5 guys before getting hit by someone's rifle stock.

I woke up in an old slaughterhouse, meat hooks impaling my arms, my head shaven and a man walking up to me. It was David Thorpe and he had two men with him wielding chains and whips. Whatever Thorpe wanted, I would never talk, I'd rather die than give any kind of secrets.

"Where is the weak spot of the new super-heavy tank?" his voice boomed in the big room.

"I'll never tell, traitor!"

He nodded and turned away while his men walked up to me and started making deep cuts into my skin. I howled in pain as they slowly made their way to my neck and then made a deep jab, nearly puncturing my jugular. They stopped and hit me with the chain, causing a diagonal cut across my chest. I was bleeding heavily at this point.

"Again, where is it?"

"Burn in hell, traitor!"

They continued making lacerations and cuts into my skin until I couldn't scream or speak. They heard a battle outside and ran out the back door. About 25 minutes later Que comes bursting in. when he saw me he had a look of horror in his eyes.

"D-Dad, is that you?"

I shook my head and he called for a medic. They helped carry me to the MEDEVAC Chinook right outside. Then I heard my son open a door, shut it quickly and then vomit all over the ground. I passed out and do not remember anything after that.

Epilogue

Peace cut short

When I woke up in the hospital I saw three men standing around my bedside. Que, Commander Ben Kelly, and the doctor. All of them looked shocked. I was on life support and had 24 sets of stitches all across my body. I took off my mask and spoke in a very raspy voice.

"Que, what happened in that shed?" I inquired

"412 bodies stuffed in a wooden meat locker. 412 POWs, most being settler soldiers. You were going to be one more addition whether they tortured the information out of you or not. If I hadn't been occupied by some gas-resistant raiders, we could've saved them."

"Que, you can't blame yourself!" I whispered.

Ben Kelly had awesome news, the second wave of the assault took Morgantown. But there was a catch. Half of our forces were gone, reduced to meat piles. They had MG-3 or MG-42 Heavy Machine guns along their trenches and in houses, as well as outdated but still capable B-17 Bombers. Those bombers decimated column after column of allied armor until they could be brought down with flak and missiles. Of the 1,500 men sent in the first wave to secure Morgantown, only 98 survived with 75 of them injured.

My son and I agreed to take a break from the military after my discharge and we bought a farm near Grafton Steel Works. We needed to fix it up, sure. But it was away from everything war-related as it was 15 miles away from the Settler-Raider Battle-Line. Occasionally we'd see the gunfire from flak guns and explosions of 5,000 lbs. bombs as well as searchlights from night battles, but no more.

The Rebuilding of the farm was hard, but with assistance from a few of Que's friends, we did it. He even installed a rocking chair for me on the front porch. However, every night Que would wake up sweating bullets and screaming, sometimes even whimpering in his sleep beforehand. During the day when he was working, he would have to walk away from doing tasks every now and then to cry. He would often cry for an hour or more, classic signs of Post-Traumatic Stress Disorder (PTSD) and I couldn't get up to help him because my body was still getting its strength back. It took two years to get back to full strength.

One day, however, when I woke up about 12 after 9, I noticed there was absolutely no noise coming from outside. Que wasn't outside working on his pickup truck. I immediately knew something was wrong. By this point, I had most of my strength back, so I bolted outside and ran to the truck. It had rained the night before so I followed the footprints for 100 feet before they stopped at the door to the barn. I grabbed a flashlight and looked around. I heard sobbing on the other side of the ruined tractor.

I turned the corner and found Que, looking at me directly with his eyes bloodshot. About a foot away was a 10mm pistol. He had attempted to commit suicide and I understood why. He began to speak,

"Dad, I'm sorry. I just couldn't take the nightmares anymore, I couldn't deal with the stress."

I kicked the gun away from him and wrapped him in a hug.

"You don't have to be sorry, I'm sorry bubs for putting so much stress on you."

47

But our embrace was cut short with the telltale sound of Willy's jeep pulling up. Que grabbed his gun and looked outside. I ran outside and saw four Raiders closing in on me. I tried to reason with them but they started attacking me. Suddenly, Que ran up and shouted,

"Leave my dad alone! It's me you want."

One left the group trying to kill me and grabbed my son, leaving me with the perfect view of what was about to happen. He chuckled and closed his eyes.

"Best start running if you know what's good for you"

He opened his eyes and they were golden yellow. The raider let go and stumbled back.

"Tell all what, I'll give you a ten-second head start so either leave now or try and fight a werewolf. ...ten...nine...eight...seven...six..."

Two of them started to back off as he started counting. Another drew their gun. One decided to try and finish me with a stab right as Que reached five. At that point he started to let himself turn into his werewolf form, his voice getting deeper as the changes progressed.

"Five...four...three...two...one, ready or not here I come, you Raider Bastards!"

He let out a howl and charged the enemies, slitting the throat of the first two. Then another started fighting. Firing his machine gun. To my shock, he bent the barrel of the gun and squeezed his head until it exploded in his hand. The other started running towards the woods only to get shot by Que's M1928 Thompson SMG.

I tried to get up, but I was in too much pain, they had stabbed me in the leg, barely missing the femoral artery. Que ran to me and treated my wound with

Hydrogen Peroxide and bandaged it up to prevent it from getting infected.

Suddenly he got up to face an MP that was running over and received a note. Que ran off, put on his uniform and gear, and rode off on his Harley-Davidson.

When Que came home about 3 days later I was sitting out on the porch, waiting for him to come back. He was limping and covered in blood. I could tell something was seriously wrong. He had this to say,

"I lost too many good men during that assault. I don't want to talk, dad."

He was actually upset that he lost men, and even lost his sister to enemy fire. The war had been won, but the death toll was staggering. Of the 136,283 men who served in the settler armed forces, one third of those men were killed, wounded or are still missing. Most of those casualties were in Raider Death Camps.

The second largest cause was the battles, obviously. But the military death toll is completely dwarfed by the civilian death toll. To this day, the exact number is unknown, but it ranges from 200,000 to 300,000 and even more grotesque and sickening possible numbers.

But the war was over, the raiders had withdrawn their forces from West Virginia and we were promised a perpetual peace throughout the State. But it wouldn't last. On December 3rd, 2051, two trains carrying 300 passengers each exploded. 506 people died in total. The Raiders did it, as the remains of the bombs had a raider logo on it. Governor Hensley gathered all high ranking officials, including me, for a meeting. During the meeting he asked us what attack plans were at our disposal. First was a push to the capital of raider territory: Houston, Texas. But that one would be very costly along a single avenue. Next was the nuclear option. That wasn't even considered. Then he asked me,

   "So Major Ryan, what are you thinking?"

I pointed out,

"Sir, there are multiple strongholds, supply depots and important towns with communications relays along the way to Houston. What we need is a fight on all fronts. We need a push to New Orleans and the Mississippi River to cut off their oil supply. Another secondary assault will push north to Duluth, Minnesota. This will prevent any ships supplying resistance movements behind our lines. Finally a primary push through Saint Louis, Missouri will push them all the way to Houston. All the while we take those areas.

Hensley smiled and said the famous phrase that would resonate through my men's minds and would be the rallying cry for the SAF.

"Serve me Thorpe's head on a plate!"

Made in the USA
Las Vegas, NV
11 September 2021